Jack Ryder

In Love
WITH A
COUGAR
Erotic Romance

WARNING

This book contains sexually explicit scenes and adult language. It may be considered offensive to some readers. This book is for sale to adults ONLY.

* * * * * * * * * * * * * * * * * * * *

Please store your files wisely where they cannot be accessed by underage readers.

Please feel free to send me an email. Just know that these emails are filtered by my publisher. Good news is always welcome.

Jack Ryder - **jack_ryder@awesomeauthors.org**

About the Publisher

4Fun Publishing, a member of **BLVNP Incorporated**, 340 S. Lemon #6200, Walnut CA 91789, info@blvnp.com / legal@blvnp.com
NOTE: Due to the highly emotional reaction of some people to works of erotic fiction, any email sent to the above address that contains foul language or religious references is automatically deleted by our anti-spam software and will not be seen. All other communications are welcome.

DISCLAIMER

In Love with a Cougar
Erotic Romance

By: Jack Ryder

© Jack Ryder 2014
ISBN: 978-1-62761-747-5

Chapter One

I started dating Veronica during the summer after her senior year in high school. We had met at a graduation party. She was a neighbor of my friend Bobby that was throwing the after commencement gala. It was a fairly tame party since his parents and several other parents were there to chaperone the goings on.

I was quite smitten with Veronica from the very start. She told me much later that she had felt the same way, but that night, she was quite aloof and played hard to get. By the time I walked her home at midnight, she loosened up a little. She kissed me on the cheek and handed me a small slip of paper with her cell phone number on it. "I'd be OK with seeing you again." She said it very softly as she kissed my cheek a second time.

Although Veronica's dad was not real pleased, her mother Gynn was very cordial and seemed to enjoy watching me and Veronica fawn all over one another from the very start. The problem with her father's mistrust seemed to be a suspiciousness based on his own misdeeds. For one, he had knocked up Gynn on their graduation night thus leading to their marriage. The second misdeed came to the surface two months later when he dumped Gynn for his 20-year-old office assistant.

The next couple of months were difficult for Veronica as she tried her best to sooth her mother's hurt and emptiness. Rather than going out on dates, I spent a lot of time with the both of them just hanging out. Helping out with the "manly chores." It was a simple thing to do and it just felt right to lend a hand in any way that I could.

By Christmas time, Veronica and I had progressed to the point that we often petted one another as we watched TV alone in the den. Veronica had very perky 34C breasts that were slightly upturned. I adored how her nipples would become erect whenever I slipped my hand up her top and fondled them. There were several times that I managed to give her an orgasm just by playing with her tits.

There were times that Gynn nearly caught us. She would suddenly be in the hall wanting to know if we wanted popcorn or ice cream or any of various other types of snacks. It sometimes seemed like she had a sixth sense as to when I was just about to get into Veronica's pants. It seemed like every time I had her just at the point that she would allow me to go further, Gynn would arrive all happy and giggly.

It was the first week in spring when I finally managed to get my hand down inside Veronica's pants. I was ecstatic when I found that her panties were soaking wet as I rubbed my finger up and down the sloppy crease in her panties. Veronica had just begun to rub up and down on the bulge in my jeans when I heard Gynn coming up the hall. I felt Veronica shudder as I pulled my hand out of her pants. She later told me that I had got her off that night. I was very frustrated when I got home that night.

When I got into bed that night, I could still smell her on my fingers. My dick got really hard as I remembered how wet her pussy had been. As I began to stroke my cock, I remembered how her body had trembled as I fingered her gash. I remembered how her breathing had changed and how she had softly moaned in a soft whisper. I remembered Gynn coming in the door after I pulled my hand out of Veronica's pants and how she was smiling at me. Then I remembered the quick glimpse I got of Gynn as I was leaving the house. Her blinds were open in her room and for a brief moment, I had seen her topless. My dick erupted as I remembered how lovely her 36C cone shaped tits had looked.

It was that same night that I had learned that her mother was really a step-mother. I had never really thought about it much since they are both Latina women. Both with the dark olive brown smooth skin. Both with long silky coal black hair and eyes that look like little black opals. It had never occurred to me that they did not resemble each other that much. Veronica is a very petite 5 foot 2 and Gynn is 5 foot 9 and a very voluptuous 36C-28-36. It had flabbergasted me when Veronica had jacket and shirt, she had me sit on the bed so she could remove my shoes and sock. I fondled her tits some more while she unfastened my belt and dress slacks.

"Oooh, look at you!" she giggled it as she pulled down my slacks. I was wearing the black nylon thong that I had worn in case I got lucky with Veronica. My dick was so hard that half of my 9-inch prick was sticking out over the waistband. "This is going to be fun," she said it in a sexy sort of tone. My entire body shuddered with pleasure when she reached out to pet my throbbing pecker. I could see my fluid ooze onto the back of her hand.

"How would you like it first?" she whispered as she rolled a condom onto my dick.

"I want to fuck you from behind, bent over." My answer came instantly. The sight of her bent over in that liquor store had aroused me more than anything I could ever remember. My mind had raced with thoughts of bending her over and fucking her right there on that counter.

"Whatever you want, lover!" She stepped to the side and placed both hands on the bed as she bent over for me.

I got off the bed and stepped behind her. "Oh God, you're beautiful," I gasped as I lifted her skirt up to her waist.

"Oh Hun, that's the wrong...OH GAAAAAAAAWD," her entire body vibrated as I shoved my 9-inch cock all the way up her ass. "Oh baby...Oh Yes...Oh Yesss," she moaned in a very deep guttural voice. "Take me, baby. Oh Gawd. Take me," she moaned even louder.

I placed both hands on her hips and pounded my cock into her ass savagely. Smack, smack, smack, smack. The sound of me slamming against her ass echoed off the walls. "FUCK ME. FUCK MY ASS. FUCK MY ASS!" She screamed as I impaled her over and over. The sight of my dick slamming in and out of her, the smacking sounds against her ass, the smell of her musky sex, the sounds of her deep pleasured moans, it all overwhelmed me.

"Oh God. I'm cumming. I'm cumming. Oh yes. YES." My dick erupted and filled the condom with my spunk. It only took a few short minutes. But now, I was a man! When I pulled out of her, it made a funny farting sound as all the air I shoved up her ass made its escape. "You were my first," I whispered my confession as I scooted up and laid down on the bed.

"You were a virgin?" Her voice sounded like it was incredulous to her.

"Yes, Ma'am!" I replied very softly.

"I'll have to make this a night you'll never forget, then!" She scooted up so she was next to me with her soft body against mine.

We had a few drinks of our whiskey as we rested. Well, Ok...it was more than a few. That was a mistake since I had never drank before and had no idea how that would affect me. According to Honey, I fucked her three more times that night. Twice, she climbed on top and rode my rigid prick and then I had fucked her up the ass again before we finally passed out into oblivion. To this day, I do not remember one minute of it. I had blacked out halfway through my second four ounce tumbler of JD. But there were four used condoms on the nightstand when I came to in the morning.

Honey was spooned up against me with her soft lovely ass pressed into me when I woke up. She was completely nude. I moved my head back a bit to glance up and down her naked body. She was the first naked girl I had ever seen other than in a magazine. I was fascinated as I watched my dick swell to life between her soft sensual ass cheeks.

"Oooooh," she purred softly as I reached around to her front and began to gently roll her nipples with my fingers. I was just about to stick my cock into her dripping snatch, but she reached down and grabbed my manhood. "No, no, baby. Not without a condom!" She rolled over to face me and gently started to stroke up and down on my throbbing pole. "Unless you have a condom stuck in your wallet, we can't go there, Baby!" My dick was already seeping precum into her palm.

She giggled when she saw the hurt look on my face. "But I could fix Mr. Happy if you like," she whispered playfully. She scooted down and rubbed my cock all over her face as my body trembled with anticipation. I will never forget how exquisite it felt as her hot wet mouth slowly engulfed my entire prick. This was my first blow job and this young woman could fit my entire shaft into her throat. "Oooooh, Honey, yesssss," my legs were vibrating and my hands were tugging on the bed sheets as she very slowly bobbed her head up and down.

Gluck...Gluck...Gluck...her throat made a slight gagging noise each time the head of my dick shoved into her throat. As she raised her head, long strands of precum and saliva oozed out onto my belly and thighs. I held my head up for a long time so I could watch every moment of this fantastic first blow job. When I was getting close to climax, she used her hand to stroke the shaft while her head bobbed up and down quickly. "Oh, Honey. Oh Honey. Oh God. Yesss!" My dick began to spasm into her mouth and she sucked even harder as each ejaculation shot into her throat.

My cell phone rang just after we had finished taking a shower together. When I noticed that the screen had the photo of Veronica, I hit the off button. Last night's heartbreak was now a blast-furnace of anger. And yet, I felt an emptiness that even this night of sexual bliss could not manage to fill. Before Honey left, she told me that she had enjoyed last night more than anything she could remember. "I'm proud to have been your graduation date!" The look on her face told me that she was sincere. She even gave me her private home number in case I ever needed some company.

Chapter Three

Mom and Dad were not too pleased when I got home all hung over and reeking of alcohol. "And where have you been, young man?" My mother asked sternly.

"Out with a friend!" I said it gruffly and I saw my dad flinch at my insolence.

Mom reached over and laid her hand on his arm as a sign to be silent. "I thought you were with Veronica." I could see the expression on her face change to concern.

"She dumped me for college!" My tone wasn't as gruff this time but still was not as polite as I would normally speak to my parents.

"Oooh, honey..." I saw her face turning to sadness. "That explains a lot!" I saw her patting his arm to tell him to keep quiet.

I left the kitchen without saying another word. My cell phone rang again as I was going up the stairs. I again hit the "End" key. I wondered why she was bothering to call. She pretty much made it clear to me that she had never felt the same way I did. What could she possibly say that would make everything OK? It was over, why beat a dead horse? I felt the anger welling up again. I opened my email when I got up to my room and felt more anger when I saw half dozen emails from her email. I deleted them all without opening. Her words would just make my heart hurt more.

When Mom knocked on my door a half hour later, I was beat. Physically and emotionally I was a wreck. Mom handed me a couple of aspirin and a mild sleeping pill. "Take these, baby, you'll feel better after you get some sleep." It did not take long before I dozed off to sleep. I did feel much better when I woke back up in mid-afternoon. Mom and I had a long talk. It was one of those motherly pep talk, sort of conversations. But I did feel better afterward. I knew that everybody has little heartbreaks in their life. But this one was mine. It hurt like hell.

There were two more calls to my cell phone that evening and several more emails that were deleted unread. The merry-go-round of emotional turmoil kept me on edge and full of anger all evening. Before bed, Mom gave me another motherly talking and one milder sleeping pill to help me sleep. I finally drifted off to sleep around 1 am.

Mom and Dad were gone when I woke up that Sunday morning. It felt peaceful in the house and for those first few minutes I felt OK. The note said that they had gone to Aunt Mary's house because she had been involved in some sort of accident. They said they might be gone for a couple of days, or perhaps a week. I was just drinking my first cup of coffee when my cell phone rang.

"Haven't you done enough?" I screamed when I answered the call. "You made it very clear that we are through!" I could hear the quiver in my voice. "You made it clear that I didn't matter!" My voice had trailed off till it was almost a whisper. I hung up before she could reply.

I felt stupid sitting in the kitchen sobbing like a little girl. It was the first time that I allowed the hurt to bubble to the surface. I had a good long cry. I was just wiping my face with a dish towel when I heard a loud banging on the front door. It was not a knock, it was banging.

"You do matter, Zack! You do matter!" It was Gynn standing at the entryway when I opened the front door. "I've been trying to reach you all weekend," she added.

After I invited her in, she informed me that she was the one that had been calling me and had sent all the emails. "Didn't you read any of them?" she inquired. My face turned beet red as I answered her.

"No, I didn't. I was afraid she'd hurt me even more." My voice was barely a whisper by the time I finished. There was suddenly a dreamy look on her face that I would begin to see a lot in the future. At this moment, I took it as a look of deep compassion.

"Oooh, Zack!" She reached forward and brushed some tears from my cheek. "I told you I will always be here for you no matter what." She said it very softly and there was deep warmth in her words. "I will always be here for you!" she whispered. Even in my pain and misery, I noticed that her nipples were poking against her tight halter top. I had a momentary remembrance of that evening I had seen her in her room topless. My dick began to swell as I remembered her dark brown nipples that looked like chocolate darts when they are erect. She placed her hand on my chin and added, "I've missed my man around the house!" She had that goofy dreamy look on her face again.

We sat at the kitchen table for over an hour. Gynn confided to me that she had thought that this might happen. "I had to give her the chance..." She suddenly stopped as if she was about to say something wrong. "...To do the right thing," she added thoughtfully. Then she told me that Veronica is much like her father. "Don't get me wrong, she enjoyed your company a lot!" Her hand trembled a little as she touched my cheek gently.

"But she let me touch her!" My face turned red as I blurted it out. Gynn bent forward to look into my eyes since I had lowered my head.

"Yes, baby, and she enjoyed that!" she said it very softly. "But in her mind it was never supposed to be permanent."

As I glanced up, I could see straight down the front of her top. Her smooth brown tits were bra less. "Oh God!" I groaned softly. My dick again became fully erect.

"I was hoping it would last long enough..." she suddenly had an oops sort of look on her face. She lifted her head and smiled as she realized that I was staring at her tits. Her goofy face was absolutely glowing. "I still want to see you, Zack!" My heart skipped a beat. My eyes were riveted to her nipples that were pressing out against her flimsy top. "I still want you to come over as often as you can!"

Gynn reached over and petted my arm gently. "I've gotten used to having you around." There was a wonderful softness to her tone. "I just don't know what I'd do without my man around!" Another heartbeat was skipped. She had just referred to me as her man! I felt a very long ooze of fluid seeping from my dick into my underwear.

"I still want you to come over and do all those manly things for me, Hun!" She had a silly grin as she winked at me. "I'll make it worth your efforts!" That goofy dreamy look on her face almost seemed to be stuck on her now. "Please say yes, Zack. Pleeeeeeze!" She whispered with a hint of a pout on her lips.

"God you're beautiful!" It just blurted out of me.

There was a twinkle in her eyes now that accompanied the goofy look on her face. "I'm so happy you think that, Zack." There was a soft loving sound to her voice. "So you will keep seeing me?" My mind was racing with the visions of her half nude body and how desperately I had wanted to have her.

"I can't imagine not seeing you," I replied softly.

As she bounced up and down in her exuberant excitement, so did her tits. I felt another long oozing of fluid as I gawked at her lovely breasts dancing in front of me. When I glanced to my lap, I saw a huge wet spot on the front of my jeans. "Oh God!" I gasped out loud. As I pretended to flinch, I knocked my coffee cup into my lap so the little bit of coffee that was left would spill on my pants. She was grinning at me with that goofy smile. "Oops!" she giggled. Her nipples were still as hard as little rubber bullets when I glanced back up at her.

The phone on the kitchen wall suddenly rang and I ran quickly to answer it. I noticed that Gynn had placed her right hand into her lap now out of sight under the table. It seemed like her arm is moving slightly as she stared at me. It took me a couple of minutes to realize that she was staring at the bulge in my jeans. "Oh God...she saw it!" I had not meant to say it out loud. "What dear?" Mom asked from the other end. "Nothing, Mom. Nothing," I whispered it.

I saw Gynn suddenly shudder as I was placing the phone back on the wall. When she reached her hand back up from under the table, she knocked her coffee cup into her lap just like I had. "Oops!" she giggled. She had a sheepish sort of grin on her face. "Now we both have wet pants!" It sounded like a sexy sort of tease.

Before Gynn left to go home, she made me promise that I would come over for dinner at 6 p.m. "I want plenty of time to get ready," she whispered. I figured that meant that she would need time to cook dinner. "I'm so happy I came over," she told me as I walked her out to her SUV. "I feel so much better about things." She kissed me on the cheek then slid into the driver's seat.

I was gawking at the wet spot between her legs as she smiled up at me. "Maybe tonight we can spill some more coffee." Her voice had a naughty sound to it as she giggled. I was sure that my neighbors could see the bulge in my pants as I ran back to the house.

Chapter Four

I felt strangely giddy as I was driving over to Gynn's house. I had made this drive hundreds of times before. But that had been to see Veronica. This time, it was her mother, Gynn, that I was going to see. It was her that I was going to have dinner with and watch movies. Would it be her body that I would be fondling tonight? I had that typical teenage boy hope that I would get her naked with the same understanding that it would probably never happen. But still...it's nice to fantasize.

Gynn had told me to dress comfortably. She had suggested loose sweat pants and maybe a sweatshirt so we would be comfortable when we watch the movies she had rented. My knees nearly buckled when she opened the door to let me in. She was wearing very short and snug gym shorts. The sort that are so tiny that the bottom half of her gorgeous brown ass was very clearly on display in the back and her pussy lips were pressed against the front so tight that I could even see the indent of her pussy crack.

Although her top was a long sleeve red and black plaid flannel shirt, the sleeves were rolled up to just below her elbows and there were no buttons on the shirt. It was just tied in a knot just beneath her breasts. But it was very loose and each time she leaned forward, I got a terrific look at both her tits. "Wow you look so hot," I sort of gasped it as I stepped into the house. I felt sort of dizzy as my mind raced with nasty thoughts of what I would like to do with her.

"I'm so happy you agreed to this," she whispered. She bent forward to kiss my cheek and I got a momentary glimpse of both her lovely dark brown nipples.

"Oh God," I sighed softly. She had that goofy look on her face.

"I love how you look at me, Zack!" She said it as she took my hand and led me to the living room.

When Gynn had invited me for dinner, I had thought that she was going to cook. I was a bit surprised when I saw a large pizza sitting on the coffee table in front of the sofa. There were also two 4 ounce tumblers of brandy. I felt a little knot in my stomach as I remembered what had happened the last time I drank alcohol. When I told Gynn that I felt funny about the brandy, she told me we could just keep it to one drink then could have sodas later.

I have to admit that I enjoyed the taste of the brandy and it made me feel very much at ease. That was good because I had felt like I was on pins and needles all afternoon as I had my nasty little fantasies about what might happen with Gynn. All of which I had completely believed were just that – a fantasy that would never happen. I fully expected to return home afterward and just jerk off like so many dozens of times before.

While we were eating, Gynn admitted that when she could not reach me on Saturday morning, she had worried about me and had driven by my house to see if my car was there. After some prodding, I told her what I had done on Friday night. I told her about Honey.

"You spent your graduation night with a whore?" The sound of her voice sounded surprised and a little hurt.

"I prefer to say she was my graduation date since my real date dumped me!"

When Gynn heard the hurt terseness in my tone, she softened a bit. "Oh, baby. I wasn't judging you," she whispered. Her hand came over and gently touched my arm. "I just thought that maybe…did you fuck her?" she just asked it straight out.

"Only in the butt and she gave me a blow job in the morning!" Because I had blacked out and could not remember the three times that I fucked Honey, it was same as if it had never happened. At least, that's how I saw it. "And I was so drunk that I don't even remember most of it!" I felt like I had told her the truth.

"Was she pretty?" The question surprised me. As a 19-year old teen, I did not know yet that all women ask these types of questions. Fortunately, I came up with the perfect answer. But that was only because it was the truth.

"Not even close to how beautiful you are!" I replied without hesitation. "No one could be as pretty as you, Gynn!" I saw that dreamy look on her face again as she reached for her brandy.

"Did you think I was pretty that night you watched me in my room?" I almost choked on my pizza. It had never occurred to me that she could see me in the mirror as I was watching her outside. "Did you go home and jerk off for me?"

I reached for my glass of brandy and swallowed the half that was left in one gulp. She was smiling at me as I set the glass back down. "Yes, I did!" I whispered my confession. "Twice!" That goofy look was now glowing on her face.

"I'm so sorry you had to spend your special night with a prostitute." she said it softly. "We'll have to find a way to make a better memory than that." I had no idea what that was supposed to mean. But I was thankful that she finally let the matter drop after that.

When we finished eating, Gynn took the pizza box back to the kitchen and came back with a soda for me and a second glass of brandy for herself. Before starting the movie that she selected on the pay per view, she turned off all the lights and lit a couple of candles on the end tables next to the couch. "This is cozy, baby," she whispered as she sat down and curled up next to me with her feet up on the couch, head on my shoulder and hand resting gently on my chest.

The warmth of her hand against my chest felt terrific. When I glanced down, I could see both of her soft upturned breasts perfectly. She had untied the knot and the shirt was dangling open in the front. My dick began to swell instantly. The movie Gynn had chosen was a love story that was about a younger woman that wanted to give her virginity to an older man. Because it was a pay per view, it had very vivid sexual situations and torrid sex scenes. Within ten minutes, the man was between her legs pumping away in her vagina. My dick was throbbing and very noticeable in the loose sweatpants I had worn.

"Is this bothering you?" Gynn had moved her hand inside of my sweatshirt as she said it. The sensation of her warm soft hand on my bare chest was sensational.

"No. Oh No!" I gasped softly as she flicked a finger across one of my nipples. Without even thinking about it, I slid my hand up and cupped one of her bare breasts and began to squeeze gently.

"Yes, baby, yes." She whispered her soft moan. I froze when I realized what I was doing. As I began to remove my hand from her breast, she pinned my arm with hers without taking her hand out of my shirt. "It's OK, baby, I want you to do that," Her lips were now on the side of my neck and she began to kiss me gently as she twisted gently on my nipple.

"Oh my God," I gasped softly as I began to fondle her. As I glanced down, it was marvelous to see my hand feeling her lovely tits. I could see a small wet spot developing on the huge bulge in my sweatpants.

"You like my tits, don't you, baby?" she giggled softly and then gently sucked on the side of my neck.

"Yes. Oh God yes," I moaned. I then noticed that Gynn had a wet spot that was growing in the crotch of her gym shorts. I could practically see her pussy lips through the thin soaked fabric.

I scooted down a bit and kissed her. At first it was just a tender kiss on her lips, but when she thrust her tongue deep into my mouth, I moaned into her mouth and began squeezing a lot more vigorously on her tits. I could feel her trembling as I rolled each of her nipples between my fingers. "I want you, Zack. I have always wanted you," her voice trembled as I scooted down and started to suck on her tits. "Yes, baby. Oh God help me. I want this," she moaned.

The sound of her moaning thrilled me deeply as I sucked and mauled on her tits. My body shivered delightfully as her hand found its way into my sweatpants. The feeling of her soft hand on my rigidness was breathtaking. My cock got slicker and slicker with precum as she slowly stoked me up and down. "I want to be your first, Zack." She whispered it into my ear and then kissed the side of my neck. "I want to be your first lover!" I felt her pushing my pants down to expose my cock. "Oooh baby. Yes!" she gasped softly when she saw my 9-inch prick.

Gynn suddenly moved over then got up off the couch. She allowed her top to fall to the floor and then wiggled out of her gym shorts. She was standing right in front of me totally nude. I could see the glistening between her legs from her arousal. "Are you sure you want this, baby?" she asked softly. "You want me to be your first?" My body was vibrating with my need for her. My desperateness to have her and be inside of her. "Oh God yes, Gynn. Yes I do. Yes I do," I gasped my reply.

Gynn had me sit up on the couch and stick my legs out so my feet were on the floor. She stepped forward straddling my legs. "Oooh Gynn, look at thaaaaaaat," I moaned lustfully as she used her fingers to spread her pussy lips wide apart. It was the most wonderful shade of pink that I had ever seen as I looked up into her pussy canal. She very slowly lowered herself down till my dick was completely buried inside of her.

"Oh...My...God...Gynn!" I groaned. I will never forget how truly sensational her pussy felt wrapped around my pulsating dick. Without a condom, the heat and the wetness of her pussy felt exquisite as she slowly began to rock back and forth. "You like that, baby? You like that?" she whispered. My entire body was quivering with arousal.

"Oh God yes. God yes. God yes," I moaned my reply. As I leaned forward to suck on her tits, Gynn placed her hand gently on my head and pulled me closer to her breasts. "Yes, baby, take all of me," she whispered.

The hot slippery fluid that was oozing out of her and running down my thighs just aroused me even deeper. I was mesmerised as I watched my dick poking into her hole over and over. For all purposes, this truly was my first fuck. I was enthralled with every moment of it. I felt her body beginning to jerk as she slammed herself all the way down on my prick. She was grinding very forcefully with my cock buried all the way inside. "I'm cumming, baby. I'm cumming. I'm cumming now!" she screamed it. As her body began to convulse, my dick started to gush deep into her sex. My legs were vibrating as I emptied all of my seed into her willing womb.

I was completely enchanted as she climbed off of me and snuggled up to me on the couch. I could see my semen oozing out of her hole as she leaned over and kissed me tenderly. "Was that good, Baby?" she whispered.

"Oooh, Gynn. I'll never forget that ever, not ever!" I replied with no hesitation. "Is it always that good?" I asked softly.

"It gets even better, baby!" she held my chin in her hand. "I want to teach you everything, Zack. I want to do everything with you!" We kissed very passionately for several minutes. Then she led me to her bedroom. The same room I had seen her half naked in so many months ago. The room that would become our favorite place.

Chapter Five

It was the day before Thanksgiving and I had not been home for two weeks. Over the last ten weeks I had spent fewer and fewer nights at home. Although Mom and Dad must have figured out what was going on with me and Gynn, they never said anything about it to me directly. They did occasionally ask if I was happy. I always told them I was better than I ever expected. Mom even told me once that she was happy that I had found someone who is so good to me. But she never did say Gynn's name.

I woke up hard as a rock that morning. The intimacy of Gynn's soft brown ass pressed against my stomach still thrills me every morning that I wake up with her. After I took my morning pee, I crawled back in behind her and began to kiss the back of her neck as I reached around to fondle her tits. "Is that for me, lover?" She giggled softly as she woke up and felt my boner in the crack of her butt. It still thrills me when she calls me her lover.

"Only for you, my love. Only for you!" I whispered back. As Gynn rolled onto her tummy, I threw the blankets off of us and climbed on top of her. "My god you are so beautiful, Gynn," I told her as she guided my dick towards her sexhole.

"Yes, baby, take me," she moaned as I pressed forward to impale her pussy with my rigidness.

"I am in love with you, Gynn." I whispered it very softly.

"Oooh, Zaaaaack. I've been hoping you would say that," it came out softly too. Her breathing was deep and slow as I very slowly drove myself into her over and over. The sensation of her soft round ass against my belly as I fucked her was marvelous.

"I want it to always be like this," I moaned as I felt the tingling in my balls that told me I was getting close.

Slap, slap, slap, slap...my belly was pounding against her rump as I rammed into her harder and harder. I could feel her body beginning to tremble as her climax also drew close. "Mom...What the fuck...What are you doing?" It was Veronica. We had not heard her come in the house, we had not heard her coming up the stairs. She had not told Gynn that she was coming home for Thanksgiving.

"Oooh Geeeeeezus!" I screamed as I yanked my dick out of Gynn. But it was too late and I began to ejaculate and three huge wads of semen sprayed all over Gynn's ass and lower back. "Oh, baby. Oh yes. Oh yes!" Gynn moaned as the sensation of my cum spraying all over her got her off too.

"How could you? How could you?" Veronica screamed as I rolled off of Gynn. "You stole my boyfriend, you bitch!" she screamed it even louder.

Gynn rolled over and sat up. She did not even attempt to cover her nudity. "First of all, I am not your mother. Remember that?" She said it very calmly. "Second, he is not your boyfriend!" She said it a little louder. "You dumped him and broke his heart. Do you remember that?" Now Gynn was yelling. Veronica looked shocked and white as a ghost. "Now, get out of my room and wait in the kitchen!"

Veronica was seated at the kitchen table when we came down to talk to her. I had put on the thick white terrycloth bathrobe that Gynn had bought me recently. Gynn had chosen to wear a very short transparent chiffon robe. Her beautiful brown skin looked marvelous through the thin fabric. Her dark brown nipples pressed through the fabric delightfully, her smooth bare gash was clearly visible too. Gynn sat right next to Veronica so she was fully exposed to her.

"You do not live here anymore. You should have called first!" She said it calmly and evenly.

"I can't believe you fucked him!" Veronica's voice sounded almost timid this time as she glanced over at me.

"I did not just fuck him, Veronica!" Gynn leaned forward so they were face to face. "I loved him too. I love him every day. I love him every night and I'm going to have his baby!" My heart skipped several beats and I felt warmth radiated deep inside me that I had never felt before.

Gynn had said that she has loved me, that she does love me and is going to have my baby. "You are pregnant?" I whispered it.

Gynn sat back up and reached over to hold my hand. "Yes, lover. You made a baby in my belly!" She leaned over and kissed me on the cheek. "I wanted to tell you tomorrow as a surprise during dinner," she whispered. After that, Veronica left us without saying much more. Gynn and I celebrated.

The End

Here is a sample from another story you may enjoy:

EROTIC ROMANCE

THE 28 DAY CURE

JACK RYDER

"HI, THERE. My name is Candice!" She had that high squeaky annoying type voice that just screams that she's dumber than a box of rocks. "But I prefer Candy!" Her huge tits jiggled back and forth as she made her way towards me at the front entryway.

"How perfect!" I chuckled. "I love eating Candy too!" The look on her face was priceless as the guys farther back in the room started laughing. The smartass remark went right over her head.

"You'll have to give that laptop to your counselor," she informed me. "No outside contact for the first seven days!" Her voice was not as friendly now.

There were eleven other inmates...er... "clients" in the house. An equal mix of six men and six women. They all introduced themselves but I couldn't tell you their names since I was not really paying any attention. I was already fuming that I had to give up my laptop and my eyes were too busy scoping out the chicks. I did remember Brittany, the little blond bombshell that was once a child star on a fleeting sitcom TV show. My mind instantly calculated that I would fuck her raw if ever given the chance. It also told me to stay away from the self-absorbed ex-star. *"Way too much baggage there!"* I thought to myself. And Candy was unforgettable in her own way.

"You better leave that for later!" One of the fellas called to me from the group of clients as I started to pick up my luggage that I had sat on the floor. "Mike is waiting for you in office number one. Since you are a day late, you better go now!" he suggested.

"Is he any good?" I asked. Mostly to see if there was any negative that I should be prepared for. There was a chorus of laughter from the entire group.

"You'll see soon enough!" Candy seemed pleased to relay that to me without any further explanation.

I followed the hallway between the kitchen and that main front room to the offices in the back. The door was partially open so I pushed it open and walked in. "Don't you know how to fucking knock?" She barked it at me and I froze in place. She is a short little bombshell with dark red hair, creamy white skin with a million freckles and her hazel green eyes seemed like they want to bore a hole in me. "Get out of my fucking office and knock first and wait for my permission!" her voice sounded like she meant business.

I had to knock on her door three separate times before she finally yelled "Enter!" I could hear giggling from the front of the house. She directed me to sit in the chair directly in front of her desk. I started to explain to her why I was a day late, but she cut me off. "Just shut up. Anything you say is going to be a lie anyway, so just save it!" The sound of her voice amazed me. It was not anger. She had said that like it was merely a matter of fact and her tone was mostly that of annoyance.

After a long pause of silence, she got a little smirky grin on her face. "Good. At least you can follow directions," she said it softly. Almost whimsically.

I could feel the heat building up in my face. This little 5 foot 2 redhead had just embarrassed and humiliated me twice in the first two minutes. And, it sure seemed that she was enjoying it. "What's your trip?" I let her hear the anger in my voice. "I remind you of someone, an ex-husband maybe?" I growled at her.

"Yes. You remind me of every other alcoholic that has ever sat in that chair." Again, her voice was calm and matter of fact. "Always late, always a story and always so offended when someone doesn't believe the line of bullshit!" She actually smiled at me as she finished her reply.

Now, I was really pissed off. But I thought it better to hold my tongue. She was going to me my counselor. It would be better if I figured out some way to get on her good side. I would need her signature to get out of this hellhole. I would need her endorsement for the court to close my case and avoid jail time. After a long silence, she gave me a list of the house rules, an itinerary for the daily treatment routine and a schedule for my house chores for my first week. I gave her a wry smile as I noticed that I was on "latrine duty" for the first week.

"You must have intuitively known that you were going to hate me," I said it with just a touch of glibness.

"Not at all," she chuckled. "I figured if I started you at the bottom, you'd have nowhere to go but up." She was equally glib.

Although our first day of "treatment" didn't officially start until tomorrow, we still had to gather in the main room after dinner for a meeting. It was mostly to go over the rules one more time. No smoking in the house, no sexual encounters allowed, no substance use allowed, no outside contact....blah...blah...blah. I found it hard to take my eyes off of Mike. Her huge 36D tits pressed firmly against her blouse and even with the bra underneath I could make out the round ridge of her areolas.

I was already fantasizing about bending her over her desk as she finished her little speech. "JAAAAACK!" Her voice shattered the dreamy thoughts. "Are you going to help me with this or not?" I had no clue what she was referring to.

"Anything you want, be glad to help!" I hastily replied. I looked at the guy next to me and he nodded towards the video equipment.

"Where did you want this equipment?" I asked tentatively. I knew I was on the right track when he nodded again. Mike was glaring at me as if she knew exactly what I had been thinking.

"We getting popcorn with the videos?" I asked her slyly with an impish grin. Even in just some jeans and a non-flattering blouse, her small little curvy body looks delicious. Her cheeks are a bit flushed now which looks cute against her creamy white skin.

"This is the no frills matinee," she replied curtly. After a few giggles, it fell silent until she loaded the video and started the program.

Although it was just the beginning of fall, it was rather chilly that evening as we began watching the two-hour long movie that Mike had selected. Since the boiler had not yet been serviced for operation, it was getting cold in the large downstairs area. Mike handed out blankets to keep us warm and then went to her office to do her evening paperwork. Mike had turned out most of the lights in the main room to allow a better view of the large TV screen. She left the lights on in the hallway to ensure we could safely find the restroom if we needed.

We were paired up so that there were three people on each of the huge sofas that were arranged in a semicircle in the center of the room. I ended up sitting next to Carol, a 42-year-old single mother of two girls. The same two daughters in their early 20s that had incarcerated her here with threats of disowning her if she fails treatment. On the other end of this sofa is Bubba. A rather large Swede whose real name is Rolf. Within five minutes after the start of the video, he is out like a light and snoring softly. As are half of the other clients in the room.

I felt a subtle movement next to me as Carol scooted over and laid her head on my shoulder. "Is this OK with you?" she whispered. Her hand slowly slid up the inside of my thigh towards my crotch.

"Yes, OK," I whispered.

In the very dim light and with the blanket covering us, no one could see her fingers slowly pulling down my zipper. I could feel my dick beginning to swell as she undid the top button on my jeans and slid her hand into my bikini briefs.

"Yesssss," I purred softly.

Carol is not the sort of woman that I would normally take a second look at. Although she is not unattractive, her age and frumpy clothes would just never catch my attention. But right now, her soft warm hand stroking my rigid prick was heavenly.

When I reached down between her legs, she suddenly let go of my cock. For a moment, I thought that I had messed up and was about to apologise.

Her hand slid past mine and she deftly unfastened her jeans and wiggled them down a bit.

"Yes, baby, play with me," she whispered in my ear.

If you enjoyed this sample then look for **The 28 Day Cure.**

Also by this Author

About the Author

Jack Ryder LOVES everything there is about sex!

When he is not involved with his "swinger" friends, enjoying a steamy threesome, or being part of a raunchy "gang bang", you can find him on first class planes, trains, and cruise ships. Traveling seems to be the BEST way to finding new and interesting sexmates for him. Sexmates. Plural. He lives with the saying "The More, The Merrier!"

He owns a successful business in New York. He writes as a hobby and also as sort of documentation of his mind-blowing sexcapades over the years. He is presently roaming around the streets of Manhattan but can be anywhere in the world too, since he travels often. So, beware! You just might be his next mate.

*"The most fun thing I enjoy when writing my stories is trying to figure out which is fantasy and which was memory. ENJOY! (Preferably with a friend. *wink*)" -Jack Ryder-*

From the Author

If you have any comments, suggestions, or would just like to get a little personal, please feel free to email me at:
jack_ryder@awesomeauthors.org

If you enjoyed any of my books then please share the love and click like on my books in Amazon.

If you write me a review and send me an email I will send you a free book, or many.
(Just know that these emails are filtered by my publisher.)

Good news is always welcome.

One Last Thing, For Kindle Readers...

When you turn the page, Kindle will give you the opportunity to rate this book and share your thoughts on Facebook and Twitter. If you enjoyed my writings, would you please take a few seconds to let your friends know about it? Because... when they enjoy they will be grateful to you and so will I.

Thank You!

Jack Ryder
jack_ryder@awesomeauthors.org

www.ingramcontent.com/pod-product-compliance
Lightning Source LLC
Chambersburg PA
CBHW071353130626
46556CB00005B/2173